Feb 2014
P9-ASE-592

Gossie

Olivier Dunrea

HOUGHTON MIFFLIN HARCOURT
Boston New York

For Ed

WWW.HMHBOOKS.COM/FREEDOWNLOADS
ACCESS CODE: BOOTS

AGES	GRADES	GUIDED READING LEVEL	READING RECOVERY LEVEL	LEXILE® LEVEL
4–6	1	D	5–6	0

www.hmhbooks.com

The text of this book is set in Shannon.
The illustrations are ink and watercolor on paper.

The Library of Congress Cataloging-in-Publication Data is on file.

ISBN: 978-0-618-17674-8 hardcover
IBSN: 978-0-618-74791-1 board book
ISBN: 978-0-544-10573-7 paperback reader
ISBN: 978-0-544-11434-0 paper over board reader

Manufactured in China
SCP 10 9 8 7 6 5 4 3 2 1
4500439419

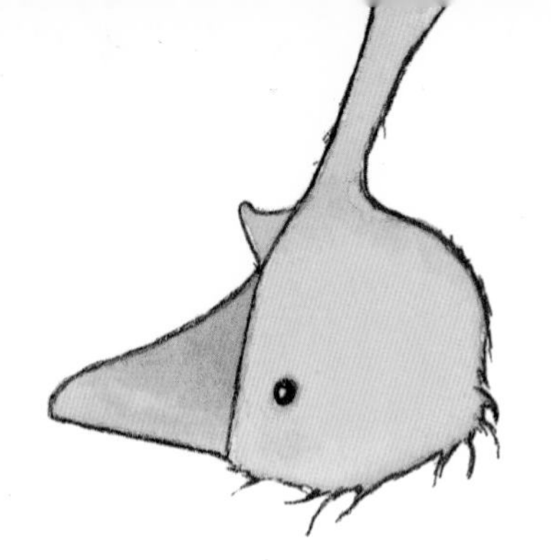

This is Gossie.
Gossie is a gosling.

A small, yellow gosling who
likes to wear bright red boots.

Every day.

She wears them
when she eats.

She wears them
when she sleeps.

She wears them when
she rides.

She wears them when
she hides.

But what Gossie *really* loves
is to wear her bright red boots
when she goes for walks.

Every day.

She walks backward.

She walks forward.

She walks uphill.

She walks downhill.

She walks in the rain.

She walks in the snow.

Gossie loves to wear
her bright red boots!

Every day.

One morning Gossie could
not find her bright red boots.

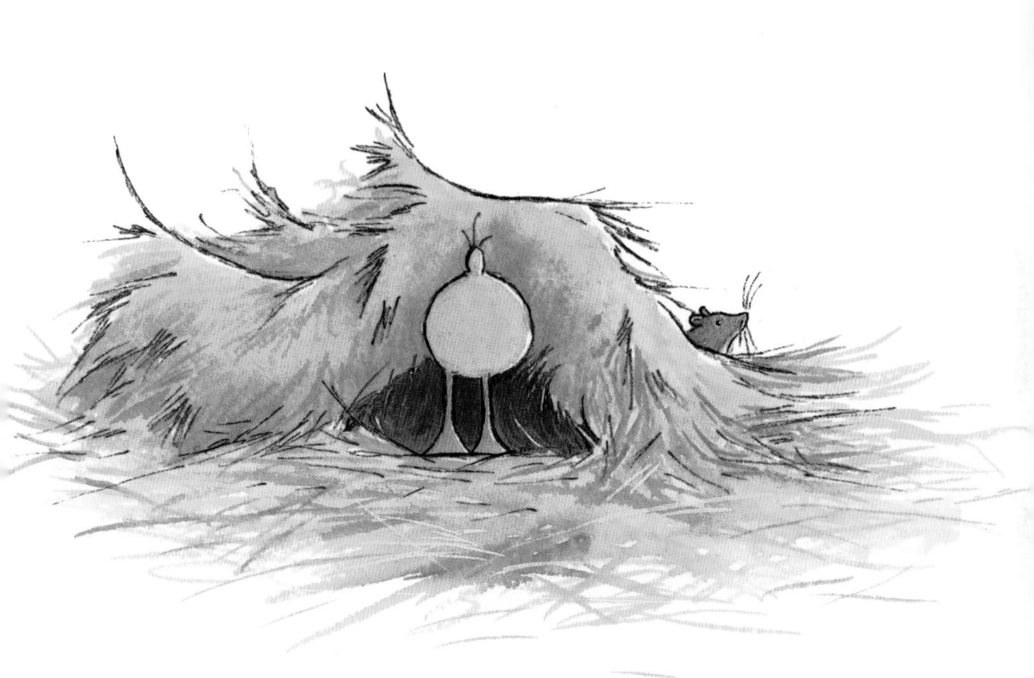

She looked everywhere.
Under the bed.

Over the wall.

In the barn.

Under the hens.

Gossie looked and looked
for her bright red boots.

They were gone.
Gossie was heartbroken.

Then she saw them.

They were walking.

On someone else's feet!

"Great boots!" said Gertie.
Gossie smiled.

Gossie is a gosling.
A small, yellow gosling who
likes to wear bright red boots.

Almost every day.